big NATE'S GREATEST HITS

Complete Your *Big Nate* Collection

big NATE'S GREATEST HITS

by LINCOLN PEIRCE

Andrews McMeel
PUBLISHING®

IF YOU WANT TO IMPROVE AT "MONO-POLY," FRANCIS, YOU'VE GOT TO PLAY HARDBALL DURING THE NEGOTIATING PERIOD!

OKAY... I'LL GIVE YOU ORIENTAL AVENUE FOR ILLINOIS AVENUE AND PARK PLACE!

THAT SEEMS FAIR...

NO! NO, THAT'S **NOT** FAIR!

WANT ME TO THROW IN MARVIN GARDENS?

WAP!

YYYYYESSS! EVEN WITH YOU GUYS TEAMING UP AGAINST ME, I **STILL** WON!

THAT MAKES **ONE HUNDRED** GAMES IN A ROW THAT I'VE BEATEN YOU, FRANCIS! I AM THE "MONOPOLY" **KING!!**

ONE HUNDRED GAMES! THAT'S **GOT** TO BE A RECORD! LET'S ALERT THE MEDIA! LET'S CALL THE NEWSPAPER!

I CAN SEE THE HEADLINES NOW!...

"BOY, ELEVEN, GETS TINY TOP HAT STUCK UP HIS NOSE."

SO LONG, DAD! I'M GONNA GO SKATING ON THE POND!

SAAAY!... THAT SOUNDS LIKE FUN!

I THINK I'LL JOIN YOU!

WHAT? UM... WELL... I'M NOT GOING TO BE THERE THAT LONG...

PLUS, THE ICE IS PROBABLY PRETTY ROUGH... NO NEED FOR YOU TO COME...

NONSENSE! I'LL GET MY STUFF!

WHO'S THE BALD GUY IN THE FIGURE SKATES?

NO IDEA.

Dave wants to drive from Boston to Washington, 460 miles away. If he leaves at 7:30 a.m. and travels at a constant speed of 60 miles per hour, what time will he reach Washington?

WHAT DID YOU GET FOR THAT ONE, NATE?

I DIDN'T DO THAT ONE, MR. STAPLES. I THOUGHT IT WAS A LAME QUESTION.

I MEAN, HOW COULD THIS GUY DRIVE AT A CONSTANT RATE OF SPEED THE **WHOLE WAY?** WHAT IF THERE'S TRAFFIC? WHAT ABOUT TOLL BOOTHS? AND HE'S GOTTA STOP FOR **GAS,** RIGHT?

...OR WHAT IF HE WANTS TO STOP AND **EAT?** OR GO TO THE BATHROOM? THEY DON'T CALL THEM "REST STOPS" BECAUSE PEOPLE DRIVE RIGHT BY THEM!

PLUS, WHO ACTUALLY **DRIVES** FROM BOSTON TO WASHINGTON? IT'S LIKE... HEL**LO**?! TAKE THE **SHUTTLE!**

WHOEVER WROTE THIS QUESTION IS LIVING IN A DREAMWORLD! REALITY!... GIVE ME REALITY!

YOU WANT REALITY?

PRINCIPAL

I'M STARTING THE NEW YEAR OFF RIGHT! I'M GOING ON A DIET!

I KNOW I'VE SAID THAT BEFORE, BUT **THIS** TIME IS GOING TO BE DIFFERENT! **THIS** TIME I'VE GOT A **PLAN**!

I'VE GOT AN EXERCISE REGIMEN! I'VE GOT A CALORIE COUNTER! I'VE GOT A DIET STRATEGY!

YOU'VE GOT A BUNCH OF COOKIE CRUMBS STUCK IN YOUR BEARD.

NATE WRIGHT presents:

Classroom CHATTER!

the o-fficial gossip column of P.S. 38!!

Well, dear readers, the entire sixth grade is talking about the new "romance" between Jenny and T.J! As of this writing, they've been going out for... ONE DAY! Wow!

Some folks seem to think it's "true love," to which this seasoned reporter says: I don't THINK so! Anyone who knows Jenny knows that T.J. is ALL WRONG for her! Class president, captain of the tennis team, honor student... WHAT is this guy trying to HIDE?

To these eyes, this relationship has about as much going for it as a stale chili dog! You heard it here first: T.J. (if that's his real name) isn't the guy for Jenny! Her destiny lies else-where... with YOURS TRULY, *Nate Wright*!

ANOTHER SHINING EXAMPLE OF JOURNALISTIC OBJECTIVITY.

T.J! HA! TOTAL JERK!

The New Craze That's Sweeping The Nation! It's...

ELLEN!
THE BOARD GAME!

Your boyfriend DUMPS you!

whatta you mean, "friends"?

LOSE A TURN!

After putting on makeup, you're mistaken for a clown!

Circus must be in town!

Go back one space!

You're constantly overshadowed by your charismatic younger brother!

ECLIPSE

Lose two turns!

You're promoted at work! YOWZA!

From now on, you'll be cleaning BOTH restrooms!

Gawrsh!

Move up three sp—

Acne outbreak on school picture day!

Move your hands, kid.

Report to dermatologist!

You bring laughter to those around you!

HA HA HA HA HA HA HA HA

BONK!

—ve back two spac—

A GAME? WHAT KIND OF GAME?

IT'S BRAND-NEW, BUT YOU'LL FEEL LIKE YOU'VE BEEN PLAYING IT YOUR WHOLE LIFE!

... AND SO NOW SHE'S GOING OUT WITH T.J! **T.J!** HE IS **TOTALLY** WRONG FOR HER!

HE'S GOING TO GO OUT WITH HER FOR A WHILE, THEN TOSS HER ASIDE! HE'S GOING TO BREAK HER HEART!

... BUT **I'LL** BE THERE TO DRY HER TEARS! **I'LL** BE THERE TO PICK UP THE PIECES!

BONK!

OH, THE SYMBOL-ISM...

THERE'S MORE OVER HERE, ROMEO.

YOU KNOW, NATE, YOUR ATTITUDE ABOUT JENNY IS TOTALLY SEXIST!

SEXIST?

YOU GIVE HER **NO** CREDIT FOR HAVING A MIND OF HER OWN! YOU HAVE NO RESPECT FOR THE FACT THAT SHE DOESN'T **WANT** YOU!

HEY, I'M NOT A SEX-IST! I'M JUST WAIT-ING FOR HER TO REALIZE HOW **GREAT** I AM! OF **COURSE** SHE HAS A MIND OF HER OWN!

YOU, ON THE OTHER HAND...

I'VE GOT THE WHOLE PACKAGE! GREAT MIND, GREAT BODY!

TWENTY SECONDS LEFT, WE'RE DOWN BY ONE, AND **I** HAVE THE BALL! THE OUTCOME OF THIS GAME IS UP TO **ME**!

I COULD PASS IT TO STAN, BUT **HE'S** MY MAIN COMPETITION FOR PLAYING TIME! WHY SHOULD I MAKE **HIM** LOOK GOOD?

THEN THERE'S RUSTY, THE MOST ANNOYING KID IN THE SIXTH GRADE! LIKE I'M REALLY GONNA GIVE **HIM** THE BALL!

DAN'S OPEN, BUT HE'S THE WORST SHOOTER OF ALL TIME! HE COULDN'T HIT THE OCEAN IF HE WAS STANDING ON THE BEACH!

...AND AM I GONNA GIVE UP THE BALL TO **T.J.**, THE JERK WHO'S GOING OUT WITH THE GIRL OF MY DREAMS? I DON'T **THINK** SO!

I KNOW! I'LL JUST SHOOT MY**SELF**!...

SWAT!

...IN THE FOOT.

YOU KNOW, COACH, SOCIAL STUDIES IS SO MUCH BETTER WITH **YOU** TEACHING IT!

WELL, NATE, I'M ONLY HERE UNTIL MRS. GODFREY RETURNS FROM MATERNITY LEAVE.

BUT NOBODY **WANTS** HER TO COME BACK!

WE'VE BEEN STUDYING THE DECLARATION OF INDEPENDENCE, RIGHT? WELL, WHY CAN'T WE DECLARE **OUR** INDEPENDENCE FROM **HER**?

THE PURSUIT OF HAPPINESS...

GETTING HER FIRED WOULD BE A GREAT CLASS PROJECT, DON'T YOU THINK?

CHECK IT OUT, COACH! THE CLASS HAS WRITTEN UP A "DECLARATION OF SOCIAL STUDIES INDEPENDENCE"!

WE'RE DECLARING OUR INDEPENDENCE FROM THE FOLLOWING: MRS. GODFREY, BORING TEXTBOOKS, ESSAY QUESTIONS, ASSIGNED SEATING, ORAL REPORTS...

GOOD GRAVY! WHATEVER HAPPENED TO PERSONAL RESPONSIBILITY?

OOOOH! **GOOD** ONE!

ADD IT TO THE LIST!

SORRY, NATE...YOU CAN'T CREATE A "DECLARATION OF SOCIAL STUDIES INDEPENDENCE" TO GET MRS. GODFREY FIRED.

BUT WE DON'T **WANT** HER AS OUR TEACHER! DOESN'T OUR OPINION COUNT? DIDN'T YOU TEACH US WE HAVE CERTAIN UNALIENABLE RIGHTS?

YES...

...BUT SO DOES **SHE**.

THERE'S A NASTY LITTLE LOOPHOLE.

"FEELINGS"
with your host: DR. WARREN FUZZY!

Today's topic, friends, is MOTHERHOOD! I'm here talking with new mom MRS. GODFREY!! How's it going so far, Mrs. G?

Okay, I guess...

I love being able to lavish all my positive attention on little Katrina! But since I'm not teaching right now, the question is: what can I do with all my NEGATIVE attention?

Without any innocent students around, I have nobody to yell at! There's nobody to criticize, nobody to degrade...

Honey, I'm home!

GA-CHING!

Oooh! Let's give these folks some PRIVACY!

"*Let's establish a* DIALOGUE"! with..... DOCTOR

WARREN FUZZY!

Dr. FUZZY counsels Mr. & Mrs. Godfrey...

Let's put some **LOVE** back in this marriage, gang!

I want the two of you to sit down on this (⁝chuckle⁝) LOVEseat and TELL each other things you LIKE about each other!

Well... I like your mustache.

I like yours, too.

Good, **GOOD**! I can FEEL the togetherness!

ook! Ack!

CLAP CLAP

YOU KNOW ONE COOL THING ABOUT CARTOONING? THERE ARE ALL SORTS OF SPECIAL **SYMBOLS** YOU CAN USE!

Of course, everyone knows that a light bulb = **IDEA**!

100 watts

3 watts

If you're sawing wood, you're snoring!

In a good mood? Use these sicky-sweet symbols!

Sweat beads and motion lines indicate **FEEAAR**

And when you're feeling down, you're LITERALLY under a cloud!

GLOOM

SLUMP

THIS IS COOL! WHAT **OTHER** SYMBOLS ARE THERE?

HMM... LET ME THINK...

THONK!

" Oh for crying out loud!
Not 'Barbara Ann' again! "

"There goes Lenny again—he thinks
he's king of all he surveys."

39

LOOK AT THAT BIG BLANK WALL OVER THERE BY THE FOOD LINE!

WHAT ABOUT IT?

IT'S JUST **CRYING OUT** TO BE **DECORATED** IN SOME WAY! I COULD PAINT A **MURAL** ON THAT WALL!

I COULD BE THE MICHELANGELO OF P.S. 38! AND THIS CAFETERIA WILL BE MY SISTINE CHAPEL!

DOES THE SISTINE CHAPEL SERVE MEAT LOAF?

I'M PICTURING A LARGE SELF-PORTRAIT...

WHAT ARE YOU WORKING ON?

MY NEW MURAL DESIGN.

MR. ROSA VETOED MY FIRST ONE! HE SAID I COULDN'T DO A SELF-PORTRAIT! HE SAID IT WASN'T RELEVANT TO OUR SCHOOL!

...SO **THIS** TIME, I'M GONNA BE **SMART** ABOUT IT! NOT ONLY AM I DEPICTING A SCHOOL EVENT, I'M ALSO SNEAKING IN A PICTURE OF MYSELF!

"FOOD FIGHT AT P.S. 38."

THAT'S ME, NAILING MRS. GODFREY WITH A PLATE OF EGG SALAD!

WHAT A REVOLTING DEVELOPMENT!

ß33

PAINTING A MURAL IN THE CAFETERIA WAS MY IDEA, BUT NOW MR. ROSA'S TURNED IT INTO A **GROUP PROJECT**! EVERY PERSON IN THE CLASS GETS TO CONTRIBUTE!

IT'S NOT **RIGHT**! THE POWER OF MY ARTISTIC VISION IS BEING **DILUTED**! I'M BEING FORCED TO WORK WITH **AMATEURS**!

DO YOU KNOW WHAT IT'S LIKE TO BE SURROUNDED BY MEDIOCRITY?

NOT SURROUNDED, EXACTLY, BUT IN CLOSE PROXIMITY.

THIS IS TURNING OUT TO BE THE LAMEST MURAL IN HISTORY!

IF WE'D STUCK WITH **MY** DESIGN, WE'D HAVE A **MASTERPIECE** NOW! INSTEAD, WE'VE GOT THIS CHEESY **THEME** FORCED ON US!

"HANDS ACROSS OUR SCHOOL"! HOW WEAK CAN YOU GET? "HANDS ACROSS OUR SCHOOL"!

PEOPLE, **PEOPLE!** CAN WE **PLEASE** COME UP WITH A BETTER THEME?

HOW ABOUT "HANDS AROUND YOUR THROAT"?

HOW CAN COACH EXPECT ME TO SIGN A VALENTINE CARD TO **MRS. GODFREY**, OF ALL PEOPLE?

THE WOMAN IS MY **ARCHENEMY!** IF I WRITE "WE MISS YOU, COME BACK SOON," SHE'LL **KNOW** IT'S A TOTAL LIE!

...BUT IF I DON'T WRITE **ANY**THING, SHE'LL HATE ME FOR NOT SIGNING HER CARD! SHE'LL NEVER LET ME FORGET IT!

WHAT IF I WRITE SOMETHING THAT **SEEMS** NICE, BUT REALLY **ISN'T?**

I CAN'T TELL YOU WHAT A GREAT IDEA THAT IS.

English Section 6-A

Assignment: Conduct an interview with a friend, family member, or teacher on the subject of his or her job.

A CONVERSATION WITH MRS. CZERWICKI, DETENTION ROOM MONITOR

Me: Hi, Mrs. Czerwicki.
MC: Hello, Nate.
Me: How long have you been a detention monitor?

MC: Well, that's actually only PART of my job. Officially, I'm a teacher aide.
Me: Whatever. How long have you been doing THAT, then?

MC: Twenty-three years.
Me: Twenty-three YEARS! Yow! How old are you?
MC: How old? Uh...
Me: What, like... seventy?
MC: NO, I'm not SEVENTY!

Me: Let's move along.
MC: Good idea.
Me: What's the funniest thing any kid ever did during school?
MC: Well...a student once wore pajamas to class...

Me: That's IT? What's so funny about THAT?
MC: Well, I thought it...
Me: What about that time I super-glued a dead fish inside the copy machine in the teachers lounge?

MC: That was YOU?

End of interview

53

I'M HANDING BACK YOUR QUIZZES, FOLKS!

COACH, WE HAVE A PROBLEM.

WE DO?

YOU KNOW THAT RESEARCH PAPER YOU ASSIGNED? IT'S DUE TOMORROW!

YES, I KNOW.

...BUT OUR BIG GAME AGAINST JEFFERSON IS **TONIGHT**!

NATE, I ASSIGNED THAT PAPER **THREE WEEKS** AGO! YOU SHOULD BE **FINISHED**!

WELL... YEAH. BUT THAT'S NOT THE POINT!

THE POINT IS, WE'VE GOT TO BEAT JEFFERSON! THEY'RE OUR ARCH-RIVAL!

AS YOUR STARTING POINT GUARD, I HAVE TO FOCUS ON THE **GAME**! I CAN'T BE WORRYING ABOUT FINISHING SOME RESEARCH PAPER!

SO WE UNDERSTAND EACH OTHER, RIGHT, COACH?

WINK WINK

OH, YES.

WE'RE WINNING!

SHUT UP.

THE WEIRDEST THING HAPPENED YESTERDAY WHILE I WAS WATCHING TV! I BUMPED MY HEAD ON THE END TABLE, SEE...

I GOT KNOCKED UNCONSCIOUS! THEN, ALL OF A SUDDEN I WAS WALKING DOWN A TUNNEL! I SAW A BRIGHT WHITE LIGHT...

I THINK... I THINK I MIGHT HAVE HAD A **NEAR-DEATH EXPERIENCE!**

TO HAVE A NEAR-DEATH EXPERIENCE, DON'T YOU NEED TO HAVE A LIFE?

THE MORE I THINK ABOUT IT, THE MORE CERTAIN I AM THAT I HAD A NEAR-DEATH EXPERIENCE!

OH, BROTHER...

I **DID!** I WAS IN THE ICY GRIP OF DEATH, BUT I WAS SENT BACK! IT WASN'T MY TIME YET!

YOU KNOW WHY? IT'S MY DESTINY TO DO SOMETHING **GREAT** IN MY LIFE! I GOT SENT BACK TO **ACCOMPLISH** THAT SOMETHING!

CAN WE ASSUME IT DOESN'T INVOLVE A CAREER IN MATH?

A **36??** DANG!

...AND THEN I FLOATED OUT OF MY BODY! I WAS IN A TUNNEL, WALKING TOWARD A BRIGHT WHITE LIGHT!...

BUT THEN SOMETHING PULLED ME BACK! YES, I WAS YANKED BACK FROM THE ABYSS!

YAWNNN

I'M IMPRESSING THESE BABES WITH THE GRIPPING TALE OF MY NEAR-DEATH EXPERIENCE!

WHAT ABOUT YOUR **BRAIN-**DEATH EXPERIENCE?

HEY, WHERE'D THEY GO?

LOOK AT THAT! IT'S SO UNFAIR!

WHAT IS?

A **SIXTH**-GRADE GIRL GOING STEADY WITH A **SEVENTH**-GRADE GUY! THOSE JERKS ARE STEALING ALL OUR WOMEN!

WHY DON'T THEY DATE THEIR **OWN** GIRLS? THEY SHOULD.... WHOA, WHOA, **WHOA! WAIT** A SECOND!

IF THE SEVENTH-GRADE GUYS ARE DATING **OUR** GIRLS, THAT MEANS **THEIR** GIRLS ARE AVAILABLE FOR **US!**

THOSE SEVENTH-GRADE BABES ARE PROBABLY **DYING** FOR SOMEBODY TO ASK THEM OUT! WELL, WHY NOT **ME**?

THERE'S A FLOCK OF THEM RIGHT OVER THERE! I'M MAKING A MOVE! I'M PUTTING MY PLAN INTO ACTION!

YEAH?

MY PLAN HAD ONE FLAW.

ONE SHORT, NAIVE LITTLE FLAW!

PAT PAT

MRS. GODFREY'S MATERNITY LEAVE IS ALMOST OVER! SHE'LL BE BACK ON MONDAY TO MAKE OUR LIVES MISERABLE AGAIN!

...SO I'M GOING TO ENJOY TODAY AND TOMORROW TO THE **FULLEST**! I'M GOING TO SQUEEZE EVERY LAST OUNCE OF ENJOYMENT OUT OF THE NEXT TWO DAYS!

SOMEBODY'S AL**READY** SQUEEZED ALL THE ENJOYMENT OUT OF THEM.

POP QUIZ, PEOPLE!

CLASS, I KNOW YOU MUST BE SURPRISED TO SEE ME HERE. I WASN'T SUPPOSED TO COME BACK UNTIL MONDAY!

...BUT I GOT SO EXCITED ABOUT GETTING BACK INTO THE CLASSROOM, I SIMPLY COULDN'T STAY AWAY!

COACH HAS KEPT ME POSTED ON YOUR PROGRESS, SO EVEN THOUGH I'VE BEEN GONE FOR THREE MONTHS, I KNOW WHAT YOU'VE ALL BEEN UP TO!

EACH AND EVERY ONE OF YOU.

OH, HOW I HATE HER...

Dan Cupid meets DAD!

an original Nate Wright comic!

Greetings, fellow fat bald guy!

Gawrsh! Dan Cupid!

You've been alone long enough, Dad! Let me pierce you with one of my "love darts"!

Ka sproing!

Now I'll go find a woman, hit HER with a dart, and BINGO! Instant romance!

Oh, THERE you are, Dan!

What's up, gang?

We're all headed over to Cloud Nine!

Yeah! There's a big party!

Ooh! I'm there!

HOURS LATER...

Come on, Dan! We're flying over to Hollywood to find a gal for Keanu Reeves!

Hmm...

What's wrong, Dan?

I just can't shake the feeling that I'm FORGETTING something!

COME HERE OFTEN?

GET LOST.

74

NOW THAT MRS. GOD-FREY'S BACK FROM MATERNITY LEAVE, YOU KNOW WHAT'D BE GREAT? IF SHE HAD **ANOTHER** BABY!

THEN SHE'D HAVE TO TAKE ANOTHER THREE MONTHS OFF!

I'M GONNA GO TRY TO CONVINCE MRS. GODFREY TO GET PREGNANT AGAIN!

IF SHE'S THAT CRABBY AT HOME, I'D SAY THE CHANCES ARE SLIM TO NONE.

MRS. GODFREY, YOU REALLY SHOULD CONSIDER HAVING ANOTHER BABY! IT'S NOT RIGHT TO RAISE AN ONLY CHILD!

IF YOU HAVE A SECOND KID, YOUR DAUGHTER WILL HAVE A PLAYMATE! THEY'LL GROW UP TOGETHER! THEY'LL BE PALS!

YOU AND YOUR SISTER ARE CLOSE, ARE YOU?

SHE JUST BLEW MY WHOLE ARGUMENT OUT OF THE WATER.

celebrity
INTERVIEW!
with: *Chip Chipson!*
Chip interviews the
month of March...

I just don't know what happened...

Three weeks ago, I was a **LION**! Sleet... snow... gale-force winds... I was wreaking havoc! I was **unstoppable**!

NOW look at me! I can barely manage a simple rain shower! I've turned into a **LAMB**! It's so humiliating!

My greatest fear is that I'll become the butt of jokes.

Now, now... No need to feel sheepish...

ODE TO A
CHEEZ DOODLE
by
Nate Wright

I think that I
Shall never munch
A more delicious
Crispy crunch.

As nectar summons
Lovestruck bees,
You call to me,
My curl of cheez.

Your taste, sublime.
Your texture, bold.
All other cheese snacks
Leave me cold.

Your color is
A fiery orange,

HOW'S IT GOING, SHAKE-SPEARE?

CORANGE...
DORANGE...
FORANGE...
MORANGE...

ODE TO A CHEEZ DOODLE

I SEARCH THE GROCERY
STORE IN HASTE.
MY GOAL: A CHEESY,
CRUNCHY TASTE.
I FIND IT, DEEP
IN AISLE NINE,
FOR JUST A DOLLAR
THIRTY-NINE.

A BAG OF DOODLES
MADE OF CHEESE.
MY APPETITE,
A SWEET DISEASE.
MY FRIENDS & TEACHERS
TELL ME THAT
I'M EATING
SATURATED FAT.
BUT THEY KNOW NOT
HOW SATISFIED
I FEEL WHILE MUNCHING
DOODLES FRIED.

I SAVOR EACH
BRIGHT ORANGE CURL
UNTIL IT SEEMS
I JUST MIGHT HURL.
THEIR PRAISES I
WILL ALWAYS SING.
CHEEZ DOODLES,
THEY'RE MY EVERYTHING.

NOW THAT'S LOVE!

YAAY!

CLAP
CLAP
CLAP
CLAP
CLAP

MISS CLARKE! HOW COME I ONLY GOT A **B** ON MY CHEEZ DOODLE POEM?

I LIKED YOUR POEM A LOT, NATE... BUT YOUR ORAL PRESENTATION COULD HAVE BEEN BETTER.

YOU MUMBLED QUITE A BIT...

BUT I COULDN'T HELP IT! I HAD A MOUTH FULL OF CHEEZ DOODLES!

...WHICH BRINGS US TO THE ISSUE OF YOUR ORANGE TEETH...

I KNOW! ISN'T THAT A COOL SIDE EFFECT?

CELEBRITY Chat!

with your host: BIFF BIFFWELL!

Hello again, friends! I'm here with today's VERY special guest... HOPSY the Easter Bunny! Hi, Hopsy!

You the man, Biff.

Hopsy, you've been hiding Easter eggs professionally for YEARS! What's the secret of your success?

Well, Biff, I don't mean to brag, but hiding eggs is an ART FORM! There's a lot of creativity involved!

You want to hide the eggs in unique locations!... Places where folks wouldn't think to look!

It's no fun for people if they find the eggs too EASILY! You've got to make them WORK a little bit!

So the object is to provide people with a challenge?

That's ONE object. Occasionally I DO have another agenda.

And that would be?

Comic relief!

SPLURCH!

I LIKE THIS NEW ASSIGNMENT, MR. ROSA! "MAKE A PAINTING IN THE STYLE OF A GREAT MASTER"!

MY PAINTING LOOKS **EXACTLY** LIKE A VAN GOGH! IT'S LIKE I'M **CHANNELING** FOR THE GUY!

ISN'T IT UNCANNY? IT'S DOWNRIGHT **EERIE!**

THAT'S JUST ONE OF **MANY** DESCRIPTIVE TERMS...

IF VINCE HAD EVER PAINTED AN ALIEN AUTOPSY, IT WOULD'VE LOOKED LIKE **THIS!**

JENNY, YOU'VE PROBABLY HEARD THAT I'M DOING A PAINTING IN THE STYLE OF VINCENT VAN GOGH!... IT'S ALMOST AS IF I'VE **BECOME** VAN GOGH!

...AND JUST AS VINCE CUT OFF HIS EAR AND SENT IT TO THE GIRL OF HIS DREAMS, **I** AM PRESENTING YOU WITH A LOCK OF MY HAIR!

AH...... **AH**.....

AHCHOO!

OOPSY.

DIDN'T VINCE ALSO DIE AT A YOUNG AGE?

I'M HANDING BACK YOUR TESTS, GANG.

poink!

96!

FRANCIS! I GOT A **96**! THAT'S MY HIGHEST SCORE **EVER** ON A MATH TEST!

I ALWAYS THOUGHT I WAS **LOUSY** AT MATH, BUT.... **YOWZA**! I MUST BE CATCHING ON!

A **96**! WOW! CAN YOU...

THIS TEST WAS BASED ON A SCALE OF 140.

140?

YUP.

...SO THAT MEANS I GOT....

A NINETY-TWO!

YOU'RE GETTING WARMER.

IN MY QUEST TO GET ONE OF MY COMIC STRIPS NATIONALLY SYNDICATED, I'VE COME UP WITH A NEW APPROACH!

EVERYBODY SAYS YOU HAVE TO DRAW **CUTE** CHARACTERS, BUT **I'VE** DONE THE **OPPOSITE**! **MY** CHARACTERS ARE ABSOLUTELY **REPULSIVE**!

TAKE A LOOK! GIVE ME YOUR THOUGHTS!

I'M NOT SURE I WANT TO SHARE A LOCKER WITH YOU ANYMORE...

GOOD, **GOOD**! HEY, GIRLS! WANNA GET GROSSED OUT?

MY NEW COMIC STRIP IS PURE GENIUS! **ANYBODY** CAN CREATE CUTESY, SICKY-SWEET CHARACTERS!...

...BUT IT TOOK **NATE WRIGHT** TO COME UP WITH THE WORLD'S MOST **REPULSIVE** COMIC STRIP! IT'S REVOLUTIONARY!

YOU DON'T **WANT** TO LOOK, BUT YOU **HAVE** TO! IT'S JUST TOO **DISGUSTING** TO TURN AWAY!

LIKE THAT TIME WE SAW MRS. GODFREY TWEEZING HAIRS OUT OF HER NOSE?

HEE HEE! MAN, WAS **THAT** EVER A LOSING BATTLE!

MY LUCKY SOCKS CAME THROUGH AGAIN! I JUST ACED THE MATH TEST!

GOOD! NOW YOU CAN WASH THOSE NASTY THINGS!

WASH THEM?? ARE YOU **CRAZY?** I AM ON A **MAJOR** ROLL! WHY DO ANYTHING TO MESS IT UP?

IF I WASHED THESE SOCKS, IT COULD DESTROY THEIR SPECIAL POWERS! IT COULD **ROB** THEM OF THEIR... THEIR...

"ESSENCE."

HEY, WHERE DID ALL THESE FLIES COME FROM?

MAYBE I'M CHARGING TOO MUCH...

YES, THAT MUST BE IT.

GOOD FORTUNE GUARANTEED! RUB MY LUCKY SOCKS 50¢

I HATE GETTING DRESSED UP! THIS TIE IS **STRANG**-LING ME!

SO YOU'VE SAID.

I WANT TO STAY HOME! DO WE **HAVE** TO GO TO CHURCH?

WE'RE GOING.

BUT **ELLEN** ISN'T GOING! HOW COME **SHE** GETS TO STAY HOME?

SHE'S GOT A TEST TO STUDY FOR.

❊ GRUMBLE ❊ NONE OF MY **FRIENDS** GO TO CHURCH...

SEE? THERE'S TEDDY! **HE'S** PLAYING **FOOTBALL**!

GET IN THE CAR.

I'VE GOT TIME FOR ONE CATCH! **TEDDY! TOSS IT HERE!**

NO, NATE! WE'RE—

WUMP!

LOOKS LIKE I'LL BE STAYING HOME AFTER ALL...

FOR ABOUT THE NEXT MONTH.

YOU KNOW WHAT? I'LL BET MOST TEACHERS DON'T REALLY **WANT** TO BE TEACHERS!

MOST OF THEM WERE PROBABLY **FAILURES** AT OTHER THINGS WHO HAD TO TURN TO TEACHING AS A LAST RESORT!

SO WHAT HAPPENS? THEY END UP BITTER AND BEATEN DOWN! THEY RESENT THEIR JOBS, THEIR COLLEAGUES AND THEIR STUDENTS!

AM I RIGHT?

AT THE MOMENT, YES.

YOU FIT MY PROFILE OF A TYPICAL TEACHER ALMOST **EXACTLY**, MR. ROSA!

AS A YOUNG MAN, YOU WANTED TO BE A GREAT ARTIST! WHEN THAT DIDN'T WORK OUT, YOU TRIED TO GET A COLLEGE TEACHING JOB... BUT **NO DICE!**

SO NOW YOU'RE STUCK TEACHING IN A MIDDLE SCHOOL, COUNTING THE DAYS TILL YOUR RETIREMENT! YUP, YOU FIT THE PROFILE!

THAT'S NOT A PROFILE, THAT'S A CHALK OUTLINE.

GUESS WHAT, GUYS!! AMANDA AND I ARE GOING STEADY!

WHAT?!

OH, THAT **DOES** IT! IT'S OFFICIAL! EVERYBODY IN THE SIXTH GRADE IS GOING STEADY WITH SOMEBODY EXCEPT **ME**!

IT'S TIME FOR ME TO SWING INTO ACTION! I MEAN, IF **JEFF** HERE CAN FIND SOMEBODY TO GO STEADY WITH, **I** CERTAINLY CAN!

CONGRATULATIONS.

ALL RIGHT, LADIES! LINE UP!

HI! AREN'T YOU CYNTHIA PETERSON?

UH-HUH.

I'M NATE WRIGHT! HOW ABOUT YOU AND I GO STEADY?

WHY ON EARTH WOULD I WANT TO GO STEADY WITH SOMEBODY I DON'T EVEN KNOW?

SHE NEEDS SOME TIME TO THINK ABOUT IT.

Dance **FEVER!**

with your "poet-in-residence":

DAN CUPID!

Dan Cupid here!
I'm (as you know)
An expert on romance!

And where's the place
Where love e'er blooms?
A rockin' 6th-grade DANCE!

A chaperone
Of sorts am I.
I float above the scene,
And watch the
Writhing bodies fueled
By sugar and caffeine!

There's Francis
Dancing clumsily
With Sheila. Ain't it sweet?

And Teddy's
pseudo-disco moves
Are really quite a "feet"!

trip!

The D.J.'s lame,
The music stinks.
But one thing can't
be missed:
The sight of
Clueless teachers
Trying hard to do
the "twist."

Here's how
to do it,
kids!

Then every head
Turns to the right
As in the door
Strolls NATE!

He's dashing!
Handsome! Debonair!
And fashionably late.

Ooooh!
Aaaah!

He saunters toward
A group of girls.
A young Adonis, he.

Let's listen
As he makes his move....

WHO
WANTS
TO
DANCE?

NOT
ME.

I **DID** IT! I ASKED ABBY WILSON TO GO STEADY WITH ME, AND SHE SAID **YES!**

I'M A BACHELOR NO MORE! I'VE BEEN GOING STEADY NOW FOR **FIVE MINUTES!**

NATE?

ABBY WANTS ME TO TELL YOU SHE'S CHANGED HER MIND. SHE WANTS TO BREAK UP.

FIVE MINUTES AND TEN SECONDS!

HERE, SHE'S GIVING YOU BACK YOUR GLOSSY.

I'M READING AN ARTICLE ABOUT "TEACHER COMPETENCY TESTING."

APPARENTLY, THERE'S A LOT OF CONCERN THAT SOME TEACHERS JUST AREN'T QUALIFIED TO TEACH!

IT WON'T BE LONG UNTIL ALL TEACHERS ARE TESTED ROUTINELY! THEY'LL HAVE TO MEET CERTAIN ACADEMIC STANDARDS TO KEEP THEIR JOBS!

PAYBACK TIME!

WE WERE TALKING ABOUT LEONARDO DA VINCI IN SCIENCE TODAY. MAN, WHAT A GENIUS!

DO YOU THINK IT'S POSSIBLE FOR SOMEBODY TO BE AN **UNDISCOVERED** GENIUS?

WHATTA YA MEAN?

I MEAN, DA VINCI WAS CLEARLY A GENIUS, AND EVERYBODY RECOGNIZED THAT, RIGHT?

YEAH...

BUT WHAT IF THERE WAS SOMEBODY OUT THERE WHO WAS JUST AS MUCH OF A GENIUS, EXCEPT NOBODY **KNEW** IT?

DOESN'T IT SEEM LIKELY THAT THERE ARE PEOPLE OUT THERE WHO ARE GENIUSES, BUT WILL NEVER BE DISCOVERED?

THERE MIGHT EVEN BE ONE OF THEM AT OUR **SCHOOL!**

HEY, GUYS!

WHAT'S UP? TALKING ABOUT ME?

LET'S HOPE NOT.

HEY, WHAT HAPPENED IN SCIENCE TODAY? I FELL ASLEEP.

AH, SHAGGING FLIES! WHAT A GREAT WAY TO KICK OFF THE SEASON!

ISN'T IT EXHILARATING, NATE? SPRING IS IN THE AIR! YES, SPRING IS IN THE AIR!!

SO'S THE BALL.

WHAT?

TODAY IS MOTHER'S DAY.

YUP.

WHAT DO **YOU** DO FOR MOTHER'S DAY? I MEAN, YOU LIVING WITH YOUR DAD AND ALL.

WELL, IT'S A LITTLE WEIRD...

MY MOM LIVES TWO THOUSAND MILES AWAY! ALL I CAN REALLY DO IS SEND HER A CARD AND CALL HER ON THE PHONE!

...BUT IT'S LIKE... I DON'T EVEN **KNOW** HER THAT WELL!

WOW. THAT **IS** WEIRD.

YEAH. I WAS SO LITTLE WHEN MY FOLKS GOT DIVORCED THAT I JUST DON'T REMEMBER MUCH ABOUT HER!

SO YOU DON'T REALLY EVEN KNOW WHAT IT'S **LIKE** TO HAVE A MOTHER!

NATE!

WHERE'S YOUR SUNBLOCK? WHERE'S YOUR CAP? IF YOU'RE GOING TO PLAY OUTSIDE, YOU'VE GOT TO PROTECT YOUR SKIN! HERE, PUT THIS ON!

I HAVE A VAGUE IDEA.

FOR LATER, I BROUGHT ALONG SOME NUTRITIOUS TOFU COOKIES!

I THINK THAT WHEN TWO PEOPLE ARE A COUPLE, THEY SHOULD SHARE MUTUAL INTERESTS!

MAKES SENSE.

WELL, GORDIE'S CRAZY ABOUT COMICS! HE WORKS AT "KLASSIC KOMIX"! HE TALKS ABOUT COMICS ALL THE TIME!

...BUT I FEEL SO STUPID WHEN I TALK TO HIM 'CAUSE I DON'T KNOW **ANYTHING** ABOUT COMICS!

SO... FIND SOMEONE TO **TEACH** YOU ABOUT THEM!

THIS IS SO HUMILIATING.

BEFORE WE BEGIN, SHALL WE DISCUSS MY FEE?

Peirce

OKAY, YOU WANT TO LEARN ALL ABOUT COMIC STRIPS SO YOU AND GORDIE WILL HAVE MORE IN COMMON...

THE **FIRST** STEP IS TO TEST YOUR KNOWLEDGE OF COMICS! SO, ELLEN......
NAME THAT 'TOON!

UMMMM... NANCY?

NO, WAIT! **SLUGGO! SLUGGO!**

IT'S WORSE THAN I FEARED.

OKAY, OUR GOAL HERE IS TO EDUCATE YOU ABOUT COMICS, RIGHT? SO LET'S START WITH "PEANUTS".

HERE'S CHARLIE BROWN WALKING OUT TO SNOOPY'S DOGHOUSE...

HOW COME CHARLIE BROWN HAS NO HAIR?

HE **DOES** IF YOU LOOK FOR IT! ANYWAY, NOW SNOOPY—

WHOA, **WHOA!** WHY IS SNOOPY ON **TOP** OF THE DOGHOUSE?

HOW CLUE-LESS CAN YOU GET?

I MEAN, WOULDN'T SHE FALL OFF?

WELL, I MUST SAY, ELLEN, YOUR LACK OF COMICS KNOWLEDGE IS ABSOLUTELY APPALLING... BUT THERE **IS** HOPE!

WE'LL PLAY A LITTLE WORD GAME TO HELP YOU SHARPEN YOUR SKILLS!

I'LL GIVE YOU THE BEGINNING OF A COMICS-RELATED PHRASE, AND YOU FINISH IT! READY?

READY.

"CALVIN ANNND.."

KLEIN.

Her Comical Life!!
EVERLOVIN'
ELLEN!

Hello again, friends! Biff Biffwell reporting!

And I'm Chip Chipson! What's new in the life of Ellen Wright?

Well, Chip, Ellen's trying to learn all about COMIC STRIPS!

Why, you ask? So she'll have more in common with her comics-crazed boyfriend, GORDIE!

She's being tutored by her brother NATE, who's a cartooning GENIUS!

And Biff... it doesn't appear to be going well.

...SO THEN GARFIELD SAYS TO ODIE...

WAIT A SEC... WHICH ONE'S ODIE AGAIN?

NATE! YOU LOOK **BEAT!**

YOU'RE A LUCKY GUY, GORDIE.

I'VE SPENT THE PAST WEEK TRYING TO TEACH ELLEN ALL ABOUT COMIC STRIPS, ALL BECAUSE SHE WANTS TO SHARE IN **YOUR** HOBBY!

REALLY? SHE DID THAT FOR **ME**?? THAT'S SO **NICE!** WOW! I REALLY **AM** LUCKY!

I MEAN, YOU'RE LUCKY SHE DIDN'T ASK **YOU** TO TEACH HER.

WHY IS ANDY CAPP'S NOSE ALWAYS SHADED IN?

The Continuing Adventures Of...
SUPERDAD!
The World's **ONLY** bald superhero with a slight paunch!

As our story opens, the mild-mannered DAD is enjoying a quiet day at home...

munch munch

Ooh! He left the 8-pin, Bo!

... when *SUDDENLY*, his solitude is shattered by a cry of...

HELP!

Hark!

With superhuman speed and grace, DAD transforms himself into SUPERDAD, defender of the defenseless!

Dad streaks to the scene, where he encounters an act of unspeakable horror!

HELP! HELP!

Gasp!

Will SUPERDAD intervene? Will he leap to the rescue?

HELP!

NO! SUPERDAD turns and walks away! Oh, the callousness! Oh, the indifference!

I SAID HELP!

NOOGIE NOOGIE NOOGIE

YOU'RE ON YOUR OWN.

145

A real cut-up!
He's
DR. CESSPOOL!

Dr. Cesspool's bi-annual evaluation...

Doctor, I am NOT impressed by your performance.

I'm afraid I must recommend that your license be suspended.

WHAT?? You wouldn't! You CAN'T!! Medicine is my LIFE!

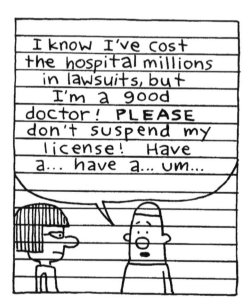

I know I've cost the hospital millions in lawsuits, but I'm a good doctor! PLEASE don't suspend my license! Have a... have a... um...

What's that big red pulsing thing called?

A heart.

WE HAVEN'T HAD A FIRE DRILL IN **MONTHS**! HAVE YOU GUYS NOTICED THAT? WE ARE **DEFINITELY** DUE FOR A FIRE DRILL!

I'LL BET WE HAVE ONE SOON! I'LL BET WE HAVE ONE **TODAY**! DON'T YOU THINK SO, GUYS? DON'T YOU THINK WE'LL PROBABLY HAVE A FIRE DRILL TODAY?

MAYBE WE'LL HAVE ONE DURING SOCIAL STUDIES...

WOULD IT KILL YOU TO JUST STUDY FOR THE TEST LIKE EVERYONE ELSE?

PLEASE, **PLEASE** GIVE US A FIRE DRILL!

YOU'RE A REAL IDIOT, YOU KNOW THAT?

ME? WHY?

WE'VE GOT A SOCIAL STUDIES TEST THIS AFTERNOON THAT YOU'RE TOTALLY UNPREPARED FOR! AND WHAT ARE YOU DOING ABOUT IT?

YOU'RE HOPING FOR A **FIRE DRILL** TO COME ALONG AND SAVE YOU! YOU'RE JUST **SITTING** HERE!

YOU'RE **RIGHT!** I'VE GOT TO **DO** SOMETHING!

SIR, NATE WRIGHT IS REQUESTING A FIRE DRILL TODAY AT EXACTLY 1:45.

NCIPAL

REMEMBER THESE, GANG?

LAST SEPTEMBER, I ASKED YOU TO WRITE OUT YOUR GOALS FOR THE COMING YEAR! I'VE KEPT THOSE LISTS UNTIL TODAY!

FOR MONDAY, I'D LIKE YOU TO CHECK YOUR LISTS! HOW MANY OF YOUR GOALS DID YOU ACHIEVE?

1) GROW SIX INCHES...

YOU'RE STILL THE SHORTEST KID IN SCHOOL.

2) LEAD THE SOCCER TEAM TO THE STATE TITLE...

WE WERE OH-AND-TWELVE.

3) MAKE THE ACADEMIC HONOR ROLL...

NOPE.

4) GO STEADY WITH JENNY...

SHE STILL CAN'T STAND YOU AND IS MADLY IN LOVE WITH T.J.

5) GET FEWER DETENTIONS...

YOU BROKE YOUR OWN SCHOOL RECORD.

6) CONTINUE TO BRING JOY TO EVERYONE I MEET, IMPROVING THEIR LIVES THROUGH THE SHEER DYNAMISM OF MY PERSONALITY.

GOOD THING I THREW IN THAT LAST ONE, EH?

RIGHT. A SURE THING TO FALL BACK ON.

NATE, WHY ARE YOU STILL HANGING AROUND?

I'M **WORRIED** ABOUT YOU, MR. EUSTIS!

YOU'RE NOT IN GOOD ENOUGH PHYSICAL CONDITION TO BE DOING ALL THIS YARDWORK! YOU'RE A HEART ATTACK WAITING TO HAPPEN!

ARE YOU SHORT OF BREATH? ARE YOU HAVING CHEST PAINS?

I **AM** EXPERIENCING A PAIN, BUT IT'S NOT IN MY CHEST.

"WHICH STATE WAS ABRAHAM LINCOLN BORN IN? ILLINOIS, KENTUCKY, OR—"

TEDDY! **DUH!** THAT IS SO **EASY!**

WHEN SOMEONE'S FAMOUS, THEY NAME A **CITY** AFTER HIM, RIGHT? SO, WHICH STATE HAS A BIG CITY NAMED "LINCOLN"? **NE-BRASKA!** OBVIOUSLY, HE WAS BORN **THERE!**

BUT... NEBRASKA'S NOT ONE OF THE CHOICES!

IT'S A **TRICK QUESTION,** TEDDY! THEY'RE TRYING TO FAKE YOU OUT!

NEBRASKA. IT'S A NO-BRAINER.

APTLY PUT.

166

★ ★ ★ ★ ★ ★ ★ ★
Celebrity
INTERVIEW!
★ ★ ★ ★ ★ ★ ★ ★

Hello again, friends! BIFF BIFFWELL here, speaking with celebrity psychic CLAIRE VOYANT!!

Well, I must say, Claire, you look different in PERSON than you do in photos! I mean... you're not SMALL... you're not LARGE...

One might say... you're a "MEDIUM"!! Get it? HA HA HA HA HA HEE HEE HYUK HYUK!

Anyway... what's your first prediction?

You will never marry.

cont'd.

MAYBE I CAN FIGURE OUT WHAT MRS. GODFREY'S LETTER SAYS ABOUT ME IF I HOLD IT UP TO THE LIGHT.

I'LL DO IT! I'M GOOD AT THAT!

HMM... I CAN ONLY MAKE OUT A COUPLE OF WORDS... UH-OH... I SEE THE WORD "APATHETIC."

"APATHETIC"! OH, **MAN**! SHE'S **NAILING** ME!

WAIT... WAIT... IT **DOESN'T** SAY "APATHETIC"

PHEW!

IT JUST SAYS "PATHETIC."

A
father's day POEM
for **YOU**, Dad!
from your son NATE

F is for the food that you are making. See the kitchen quickly fill with smoke.

FOOM!

A is for the aspirin you are taking as you pay the bills and see we're broke.

10¢

Dang! HELP!

T is for the treadmill in our cellar. You used it once, then claimed you'd hurt your heel.

H·E·R spells "her," a woman stellar. Will you ever date one? Let's get real.

HEY, DAD! WHAT RHYMES WITH "BALD"?

WHY CAN'T I HAVE A KID WHO JUST BUYS ME A TIE?

happy father's day!

pat pat

COME **ON**, FRANCIS! WHAT ELSE DOES MRS. GODFREY'S LETTER SAY?

KEEP YOUR SHIRT ON, NATE! THIS IS A FLASH-LIGHT, NOT AN X-RAY MACHINE!

I CAN MAKE OUT A FEW MORE WORDS... "EFFORT"... "ATTENDANCE".. "SUMMER"... HMMM... WHAT'S THIS WORD AFTER "SUMMER"?

"SCHOOL"

SUMMER SCHOOL!

NYAA!

MRS. GODFREY IS SUGGESTING THAT YOU ATTEND SUMMER SCHOOL.

"SUGGESTING"! IS THAT WHAT IT SAYS? "SUGGESTING"?

AH-**HA!** SO I DON'T **HAVE** TO GO! SHE **WANTS** ME TO GO, BUT SHE CAN'T **MAKE** ME GO!

SHE CAN WITH THE SIGNATURE OF A PARENT OR GUARDIAN.

ANYTHING I CAN GET YOU?

A PEN.

73.4!
73.4!

THAT WAS MY AVERAGE IN SOCIAL STUDIES! **73.4!**

EVEN THOUGH I WAS **RIGHT** 73.4 PERCENT OF THE TIME, I HAVE TO GO TO **SUMMER SCHOOL!**

THINK ABOUT IT! 73.4! THAT'S LIKE HAVING A .734 BATTING AVERAGE!

IF I HAD A .734 BATTING AVERAGE, I'D BE IN THE **HALL OF FAME!** I'D BE THE GREATEST BASEBALL PLAYER **EVER!**

BASEBALL AIN'T SOCIAL STUDIES.

STRIKE ONE!... STRIKE TWO!... STRIKE THREE!

...ALTHOUGH I **DO** SEE SIMILARITIES!

SHUT UP.

THERE GOES TERRI, THE MOST POPULAR GIRL IN SCHOOL! WHAT A COUP IF I COULD GET **HER** TO SIGN MY YEARBOOK!

TERRI! WILL YOU SIGN MY YEARBOOK? HUH? PLEASE? WILL YOU? PLEEEEEZ?

I DIDN'T WANT TO HURT HER FEELINGS, BUT THAT'S THE LAMEST SMILEY FACE I'VE EVER SEEN.

The One and Only...

DR. CESSPOOL!

a *Nate Wright* comic

His license to practice medicine suspended, Dr. Cesspool works at a restaurant!

Here's your sushi, folks!

Would you like me to expertly cut it up for you? After all, I **AM** a temporarily unlicensed surgeon!

Okay!

I wield this knife with the same skill and precision with which I used to employ a scalpel!

SAW!
HACK!
CHOP!
CHONK!

Oh, how I long for those days!

Me too...

I think you're supposed to use the **SHARP** end...

The HAPPY ENDING!

DR. CESSPOOL!

The EPILOGUE!!

So your license to practice medicine has been RESTORED?

Yup! It's been a rough time, but it was **GOOD** for me!

Emergency Room

Working as a waiter, I got to spend time with **REAL PEOPLE**! I found out that they're **INTIMIDATED** by doctors! They're in **AWE** of us! That's not good!

When I treat people, I want them to see me as a **REGULAR GUY**! I don't want them to think of me as a doctor!

Well, I know **I** don't think of you as a doctor!

Now, nurse, enough of your flattery!

Hi! What seems to be the problem?

Emer Roo

193

WELCOME, PEOPLE, TO SUMMER SCHOOL.

THE MATERIAL YOU'LL BE STUDYING IS THE SAME MATERIAL YOU **NEGLECTED** TO STUDY DURING THE REGULAR YEAR.

OUR GOAL DURING THE NEXT FOUR WEEKS IS TO VIGOROUSLY **REVISIT** THAT MATERIAL.

I'M ABOUT TO REVISIT MY BREAK- FAST.

NATE, MOVE UP HERE TO THE FRONT WHERE I CAN SEE YOU.

OUR GOAL DURING THE NEXT FOUR WEEKS, PEOPLE, IS TO HELP YOU REALIZE YOUR ACADEMIC POTENTIAL!

FORTUNATELY, THERE AREN'T TOO MANY OF YOU, WHICH MEANS...

...**LOTS** OF INDIVIDUAL ATTENTION FOR EACH AND EVERY ONE OF YOU!

OH, GOODY. INDIVIDUAL ATTENTION.

NATE! **YOU** LOOK EAGER TO START!

MOST STUDENTS ARE CAPABLE OF DOING GOOD WORK, BUT MANY HESITATE TO ASK FOR HELP WHEN THEY NEED IT!

AS A RESULT, SOME STUDENTS GET OVER-LOOKED DURING THE SCHOOL YEAR! THEY SLIP THROUGH THE CRACKS!

IN SUMMER SCHOOL, WE WORK TO REVERSE THAT! WE DON'T WANT A **SINGLE STUDENT** TO SLIP THROUGH THE CRACKS!

NOTICE SHE SAID NOTH-ING ABOUT SLIPPING THROUGH A **WINDOW**...

NATE!

MRS. GODFREY, THIS ASSIGNMENT YOU GAVE ME IS **TOTALLY** UNFAIR!

IT'S **HUGE!** FINISHING THIS THING IS GOING TO TAKE ME ALL **SUMMER!**

SAY, **HERE'S** A THOUGHT: PERHAPS THAT'S WHY THEY CALL IT "**SUMMER**" SCHOOL!

A SARCASTIC TEACHER IS ESPECIALLY TOUGH TO TAKE ON A NINETY-DEGREE DAY IN JULY...

BATTER UP!

OH **HO!** LOOK WHO'S UP! **T.J.!** THE GUY WHO STOLE JENNY AWAY FROM ME!

GET A LOAD OF MISTER SUPERSTAR HERE! HE THINKS HE'S SO GREAT!

WELL, HERE'S MY CHANCE TO SHOW THE WORLD THAT **I** AM THE BETTER MAN!

LET'S SEE... I COULD MAKE HIM LOOK BAD WITH MY DEVASTATING KNUCKLE-CURVE...

I COULD OVERPOWER HIM WITH MY AWESOME FAST-BALL... OR RING HIM UP WITH MY AMAZING SLIDER...

I COULD BLOW MY SPLIT-FINGER BY HIM... BAFFLE HIM WITH MY CHANGE-UP...

YES, I COULD **HUMILIATE** HIM IN ANY ONE OF A DOZEN WAYS!

zing!

PLUNK!

...BUT I'M JUST NOT THAT KIND OF GUY!

OW!

206

HERE COMES ANGIE. I'VE ONLY SPOKEN TO HER FOR **FIVE MINUTES**, BUT I CAN'T STOP THINKING ABOUT HER!

I WONDER IF SHE LIKES ME?...I NEED A **SIGN**, THAT'S WHAT I NEED! SOMETHING TO SHOW ME THAT SHE AND I JUST MIGHT BELONG TOGETHER!

I CAN'T BELIEVE THIS CAFETERIA DOESN'T SELL "CHEEZ DOODLES"! WHAT AN OUTRAGE!

KA- **CHING!**

SHE OFFERED ME CHEEZ **NIPS!** AS IF THEY'RE THE SAME **THING!**

Dear Grandma,

Sorry I have not written to you lately. The reason for that is: I am stuck in <u>summer school</u> and have been totally busy. What a drag.

Sigh.. Me

Wheee!

HA HA

frolicksome friends →

"How did a genius like Nate end up in summer school?" you are probably asking. Well, that is the eternal question. What an **INJUSTICE**!

(note: out of place)

Of course, the person behind this whole sorry episode is Mrs. Godfrey. Her personal vendetta against me CONTINUES!

Yikes!

She is still the same as she was the last time I wrote you. She picks on me, she yells at me, she claims I don't pay attention in class.

evil eye in back of head

It is so unfair. The woman totally **HATES** me! Why she constantly singles ME out for criticism, I have no idea.

TIME, PEOPLE! HAND IN THOSE TESTS!

Well, gotta go...

WE BOTH LOVE CHEEZ DOODLES, WE BOTH LOVE CARTOONING... YOU AND I HAVE SO MUCH IN COMMON, NATE!

I THOUGHT MAYBE THAT BECAUSE YOU'RE A TUTOR, YOU MIGHT BE A LITTLE SNOBBY... BUT YOU'RE **NOT!**

YOU'RE JUST A NICE, NORMAL GUY! YOU DON'T SEEM LIKE A TUTOR AT **ALL!**

IRONIC, ISN'T IT?

HEY, HOW COME YOU DON'T HANG OUT WITH ANY **OTHER** TUTORS?

THIS IS **RIDICULOUS!** FIRST ANGIE THINKS I'M HERE AT SUMMER SCHOOL AS A **TUTOR**, AND THEN I GO AND TELL HER I'M A **DETENTION MONITOR!**

I CAN'T LET THIS GO ON! I'VE GOT TO BE **HONEST!** I'VE GOT TO FIGURE OUT A WAY TO LET HER KNOW THE **TRUTH!**...

...BEFORE SOMEBODY ELSE DOES.

HE TOLD YOU **WHAT?**

...SO YOU'RE **NOT** A TUTOR?

UM... NO.

I **STARTED** TO TELL YOU THE TRUTH, BUT WHEN YOU JUST ASSUMED I WAS A TUTOR... I... WELL, I JUST CHICKENED OUT!

I SUPPOSE YOU'RE NOT A DETENTION MONITOR, EITHER, HUH?

ER... NOPE.

BUT YOU SAID EVERYONE CALLS YOU "MISTER DETENTION."

THAT PART'S TRUE!

HI, GUYS! WHAT'S UP?

WE JUST DID MRS. WINSLOW'S LAWN.

HOW MUCH DID SHE PAY?

THE USUAL... FIFTEEN BUCKS.

FIVE BUCKS FOR EACH OF US, EH?

WHAT? "US"?

THIS MONEY'S **OURS**, NATE! **YOU** WERE SITTING IN **SUMMER SCHOOL** WHILE "N.F.T. YARDCARE" WAS **WORKING**!

HEY, THE "N" IN "N.F.T. YARDCARE" STANDS FOR **NATE**, IN CASE YOU FORGOT!

SO DOES THAT MEAN YOU SHOULD BE PAID FOR WORK YOU DIDN'T DO?

WELL, WHEN PEOPLE MISS WORK BECAUSE THEY'RE SICK, THEY STILL GET PAID!

THAT'S **DIF-**FERENT!

NO, IT'S **NOT**! WE'VE ALWAYS SHARED OUR PROFITS **EVENLY**!

I DESERVE MY CUT! **GIVE ME MY CUT!**

HOW'D YOU GET ALL THESE CUTS?

LAWN-MOWER ACCIDENT.

WELL, I GUESS NOW WE KNOW THAT WE LIKE EACH OTHER...

IT'S OFFICIAL!

...OR IT **WILL** BE OFFICIAL, ONCE I SLIP A CERTAIN LITTLE ITEM ONTO YOUR FINGER!

YOU GOT ME A **RING**?

EVEN BETTER! A CHEEZ DOODLE!

CALL ME A HOPE-LESS ROMANTIC!

I'LL JUST CALL YOU "HOPELESS."

BASEBALL IS A GAME OF **DECISIONS!**

EACH GAME, EACH INNING CONSISTS OF **DOZENS** OF DECISION-MAKING SITUATIONS!

THE CHALLENGE IS TO MAKE THE **RIGHT** DECISION!

MENTAL PREPARATION! THAT'S **KEY!** YOU'VE GOT TO CONSTANTLY ASK YOURSELF: "WHAT WILL I DO IF THE BALL IS HIT TO **ME**?"

THEN IT BECOMES SECOND NATURE TO MAKE THE RIGHT DECISION IN A **SPLIT SECOND!**

CRAK!

TRIP!

SELECT ONE:

A.) PICK SELF UP, DUST SELF OFF.
B.) ADMIT MISTAKE, MOVE ON.

C.) FAKE INJURY, SAVE FACE.

OOOOOH...

YOU OKAY, MAN?

OKAY, SO YOU'RE GOING OUT WITH ANGIE... BUT WHAT ABOUT **JENNY?** YOU'VE HAD A CRUSH ON **HER** SINCE THE **THIRD GRADE!**

I'M OVER HER.

NO, YOU'RE **NOT**, NATE! I **KNOW** YOU STILL LIKE JENNY! THIS GIRL ANGIE MAY BE VERY NICE, BUT YOU'VE ENDED UP WITH HER ON THE —

TONG!

...REBOUND.

HEADS UP!

FRANCIS, I'D LIKE YOU TO MEET MY GIRLFRIEND, ANGIE! ANGIE, THIS IS FRANCIS, MY BEST FRIEND!

HI!

FRANCIS AND I HAVE LIVED NEXT TO EACH OTHER FOR **ELEVEN YEARS!** WE'VE BEEN ON THE SAME TEAMS! WE'VE RIDDEN THE SAME BUS!

WE'VE EVEN HAD THE SAME **BABY-SITTERS!** IT JUST SEEMS LIKE... OF **COURSE** WE'D BE BEST FRIENDS! WE JUST **HAD** TO BE!

IT WAS... **DESTINY!**

WHAT'S **YOUR** EXCUSE?

"FEELINGS"

with your host:

Dr. Warren Fuzzy

Greetings, friends! You know, we spend so much time exploring our **INNER** lives that we sometimes forget to examine what's on the **SURFACE!**

Yes, the way we **LOOK** can often hold the key to how we **FEEL** about ourselves!

Specifically, an outrageous appearance sometimes masks an emotional life in **TURMOIL!**

Dennis Rodman →

That's right! Crazy clothes and over-the-top outfits are much **MORE** than a simple fashion statement!...

They're a **CRY FOR HELP!** These poor souls need our compassion! Our understanding! Our companionship!

BEACH?

YOU'RE ON YOUR OWN.

WELL, ANGIE, I THINK THAT YOU AND NATE MAKE A GREAT COUPLE!

YOU HAVE A LOT IN COMMON, YOU REALLY LIKE SPENDING TIME TOGETHER, AND NATE'S OBVIOUSLY **CRAZY** ABOUT YOU!

HE'S BEEN SO TOTAL-LY IN LOVE WITH JENNY FOR SO LONG, I THOUGHT HE'D **NEVER** LIKE ANY-ONE ELSE, BUT...

WHO'S JENNY?

OOPS.

WAP!

WELL, NATE DEFINITELY HAS A GIRLFRIEND... SO WHY HASN'T HE **TOLD** ME ABOUT HER? WHY IS HE BEING SO SECRETIVE?

WAIT A MINUTE! WHAT KIND OF FATHER **AM** I? HE'S PROBABLY JUST WAITING FOR ME TO ASK HIM! THEN HE'LL OPEN UP!

WHAT'S NEW, SON?

NOTHING.

ANY... EXCITING PEOPLE IN YOUR LIFE?

RIGHT NOW, DEFINITELY NOT.

NATE, I'M YOUR FATHER. I AM **INTERESTED** IN YOUR LIFE!

I'VE BEEN THERE FOR ALL THE "FIRSTS" IN YOUR LIFE: YOUR FIRST WORD, YOUR FIRST STEP, YOUR FIRST DAY OF SCHOOL... AND NOW, YOU HAVE YOUR FIRST GIRLFRIEND!

I DON'T WANT TO MEDDLE, BUT I **DO** WANT TO KNOW HOW YOU'RE DOING! WHAT CAN YOU TELL ME ABOUT THIS YOUNG LADY? WHEN CAN I MEET HER?

LET'S DO THIS ANOTH-ER TIME.

TALK TO ME!

WELL, ANGIE, I REALLY APPRECIATE THE CHANCE TO MEET YOU!

I'M SURE THERE ARE THINGS YOU'D RATHER BE DOING! I KNOW HANGING OUT WITH GROWN-UPS ISN'T WHAT YOU KIDS ARE "INTO."

THERE'S NOTHING WORSE THAN BEING STUCK WITH A PARENT WHO DOESN'T KNOW WHEN TO GET OUT OF THE WAY!

YES, THAT **IS** ANNOYING.

WELL, ENOUGH CHIT-CHAT! LET'S **DO** SOMETHING!

TIME OUT. I NEED TO TALK TO THE PITCHER.

LISTEN, BUDDY... MY NEW GIRLFRIEND'S HERE AT THE GAME, AND I WANT TO IMPRESS HER, IF YOU GET MY DRIFT...

I'LL GO GET READY, AND YOU MAKE ME LOOK GOOD, OKAY? GIVE ME A NICE FAT ONE, RIGHT DOWN THE PIKE! OKAY? THANKS, MAN!

doof!

WHAT? OH, **NO**! COACH IS GIVING ME THE "BUNT" SIGN!

I TOLD ANGIE I WAS GOING TO HIT A HOME RUN FOR HER! I CAN'T LET HER SEE ME **BUNT** MY WAY ON LIKE A TOTAL WUSS! I'M SWINGIN' AWAY!

STEEEEERIKE!

USUALLY, I **DREAD** THE FIRST DAY OF SCHOOL, BUT **THIS** YEAR IS **DIFFERENT!**

WHY? BECAUSE NOW I'VE GOT A **GIRL-FRIEND!** THAT GIVES ME A **MAJOR** BOOST UP THE SOCIAL LADDER!

WHEN YOU'RE PART OF A COUPLE, YOU BE-COME MORE POPULAR! JUST THINK OF WHAT GOING STEADY WITH ANGIE WILL DO FOR MY REPUTATION!

THINK OF WHAT IT'LL DO FOR **HERS.**

EXACTLY! LIKE DAT-ING **ME** ISN'T **ENOUGH** OF A FRINGE BENEFIT!

YOU'VE GOT MR. ROSA... I'VE GOT MRS. GODFREY.

DANG! WE'RE IN DIFFERENT HOMEROOMS!

THAT MEANS WE'LL ONLY SEE EACH OTHER DURING RECESS AND LUNCH!

WAIT! MAYBE THERE'S A SIMPLE SOLUTION!

YOU COULD ASK TO SWITCH INTO MRS. GODFREY'S HOMEROOM!

COMING UP: OUR FIRST FIGHT.

ARE YOU OKAY? YOU LOOK A LITTLE PALE...

WHAT A **DRAG**! ANGIE AND I ARE IN DIFFERENT HOMEROOMS!

WE DON'T HAVE ANY CLASSES TOGETHER, WE BARELY SEE EACH OTHER ALL DAY LONG...

NOT ONLY THAT, SHE COULD FALL IN LOVE WITH SOMEBODY IN HER HOMEROOM AND YOU'D BE POWERLESS TO STOP IT!

IT'S FUN MESSING WITH HIS HEAD!

NOT TO MENTION HIS HAIR!

WELL, THIS IS ABSOLUTELY THE LAST TIME I TAKE THE KIDS TO A BALL GAME!

FIFTEEN BUCKS FOR PARKING... TWENTY-DOLLAR SEATS... NOT TO MENTION THE OUT-RAGEOUS FOOD PRICES!

PLUS, THE HOME TEAM'S LOSING BY EIGHT RUNS!

THE NEXT TIME I — OH, FOR **PETE'S SAKE!**

I JUST DUMPED MY CHILI DOG ALL OVER MY LAP!

WELL, THAT'S PAR FOR THE COURSE! WHAT ELSE COULD HAPPEN TO MAKE THIS DAY WORSE?

HEY, DAD! CHECK OUT THE JUMBO-TRON!

HUH?

COLA

ACME

258

HAVE YOU SEEN ALL THE GUYS IN THIS SCHOOL WHO ARE DROOLING OVER ANGIE? IT'S DIS-**GUSTING!**

SHE'S **MY** GIRLFRIEND! BUT THEY WON'T STOP FLIRTING WITH HER! THEY FLOCK AROUND HER LIKE MOTHS TO A FLAME!

IT'S NOT RIGHT! WHY SHOULD ANGIE HAVE TO DEAL WITH SO MANY ANNOYING LOSERS?

YOU'D THINK **ONE** WOULD BE ENOUGH!

RIGHT! I... **HEY!**

NATE, IT SOUNDS LIKE YOU'RE ASKING ME TO SPY ON ANGIE FOR YOU.

SPY? **NO!** PERISH THE THOUGHT!

IT'S JUST THAT... WELL... SHE'S **NEW** HERE! I WANT TO MAKE SURE SHE'S OKAY! I'M THINKING OF **HER!**

HOW VERY NOBLE OF YOU.

EXACTLY! THAT'S ME! NOBLE! LOOKING OUT FOR THE WELFARE OF MY GIRL-FRIEND!

I SUGGEST YOU LOOK OUT FOR IT SOMEWHERE ELSE.

LET'S GO OVER YOUR SEATING PLAN. ANGIE JUST CAN'T THRIVE SITTING NEAR BOYS.

EVER SINCE I STARTED GOING OUT WITH ANGIE, IT'S LIKE... I FEEL ALL **INSECURE** AND STUFF!

I'M ALWAYS WONDERING IF SHE STILL LIKES ME... I GET ALL FREAKED OUT IF SHE TALKS TO OTHER GUYS... AND I SIT AROUND WORRYING THAT SHE'S GONNA **DUMP** ME!

AT WHAT POINT IN A RELATION-SHIP DOES ALL THAT END?

I HAD TO BE HONEST.

DOWN TO THE ENDLINE AND BACK, FAST AS YOU CAN! ...GO!

UH... NATE?

YEAH, COACH?

ANY REASON YOU'RE NOT DOING WIND SPRINTS?

YEAH! I'M THE GOALIE!

DURING A **GAME**, A GOALIE DOESN'T HAVE TO SPRINT! MOST OF THE TIME HE'S JUST STANDING AROUND!

AH. SO THEN, WHY SPRINT DURING **PRACTICE?**

RIGHT!

IN FACT, WHY NOT JUST RELAX AND **LIE DOWN?**

NOW YOU'RE TALKIN', COACH! DON'T MIND IF I DO!

NOT ON YOUR BACK.

TWENTY-NINE...

OOF!

NOW THAT I'M GOING STEADY WITH ANGIE, I'M NOT SURE I'LL BE ABLE TO BE ON THE CHESS TEAM ANYMORE!

CHESS IS A GAME OF **WAR!** I'M TOO HAPPY WITH ANGIE TO THINK ABOUT CAPTURING AND ATTACKING! I JUST CAN'T GET **MEAN** ENOUGH ANYMORE!

SPEAKING OF ANGIE, I JUST SAW MARK JAMESON HITTING ON HER IN THE LIBRARY.

CHECK-MATE.

CHESS IS ALSO A GAME OF CUNNING.

HOW'S YOUR REPORT ON PICASSO GOING, NATE?

AWESOME, I MUST SAY!

I'M NOT REALLY THAT CRAZY ABOUT THE GUY'S ARTWORK, BUT THERE'S PLENTY OF **OTHER** STUFF TO WRITE ABOUT!

PICASS

CHECK OUT MY ROUGH DRAFT!

"PABLO PICASSO: BABE MAGNET."

A GOOD TITLE REALLY SETS A TONE, DON'T YOU THINK?

Time Once Again To Play...
"WHO THE HECK AM I?"
★ ☆ ★ ☆ ★ ☆ ★ ☆ ★
America's FAVORITE Game Show!!

...with your host: **KEN DOLITTLE!!**

Hello again, folks! Let's welcome our celebrity panel **AND**... our first **MYSTERY GUEST!**

APPLAU

Hi, Ken.

LORETTA SWIT | VANILLA ICE | MANUTE BOL

Now, Mystery Guest... Give us some clues to help unlock your **SECRET IDENTITY!**

Well, Ken... I'm 15 years old... I have bleached-blonde hair...

Mmm Hmm... Any other identifying features?

Uh... do pimples count?

HA! HA! HA! HA!

;Chuckle!; Ah-HA! Our Mystery Guest has a **sense of humor!**

Not really. But I **DO** often say things that are UNINTENTIONALLY funny due to my lack of intelligence and lame social skills!

VERY interesting! Okay, let's move on! How would your **FRIENDS** describe you?

Friends?

HA HA! **WOW!** Are you as stumped as I am, panel? This is one of the most **BAFFLING** Mystery Guests we've ever **HAD!**

GUESS WHO.

UH-OH...

IF MY ART-WORK LOOKS DIFFERENT THIS YEAR, MR. ROSA, THERE'S A **REASON** FOR IT!

YOU SEE, I HAVE A **GIRLFRIEND** NOW! OBVIOUSLY, THAT'S CHANGED THE WAY I LOOK AT THE WORLD!

I HAVE A MORE POSITIVE VIEWPOINT! MY ART NOW REFLECTS A MORE CONTENTED PHILOSOPHY!

SO THAT'S WHY ALL THOSE MAGGOTS ARE PINK?

CALL ME MISTER SENSI-TIVITY!

WHAT'S UP?

I'M WAITING FOR THE BATHROOM... BUT DAD'S IN THERE SHAVING.

IT'S TAKING HIM **FOREVER!** WHAT COULD BE TAKING HIM SO LONG?

MAYBE HE'S SHAVING HIS BACK!

WHAT THIS HOUSE NEEDS IS A LITTLE SOUNDPROOFING.

I'M GOING TO BE **RICH!**

YES, SO YOU'VE SAID.

BUT **THIS** TIME, I CAN'T MISS! I'M GOING TO BECOME A **ROMANCE NOVELIST!**

ROMANCE NOVELIST?

YEAH! THOSE BOOKS SELL **MILLIONS** OF COPIES! AND ALL YOU NEED TO SUCCEED ARE A FEW LOVE SCENES, AN EYE-CATCHING COVER, AND A TITLE!

"BELLES-A-POPPIN': A TALE OF LUST AND LOSS IN THE DEEP SOUTH."

THINK A SIX-FIGURE ADVANCE IS TOO MUCH TO HOPE FOR?

MY ROMANCE NOVEL, "BELLES-A-POPPIN': A TALE OF LUST AND LOSS IN THE DEEP SOUTH," IS GONNA BE A BEST-SELLER!

BUT WHAT DO **YOU** KNOW ABOUT "LUST AND LOSS"?

MMMF!.. ♡ MMMMM

MMMF!.. SMAK ♡

♡

✳ SIIIIIGH..✳

ANY OTHER QUESTIONS?

HERE'S THE SYNOPSIS OF MY ROMANCE NOVEL! THIS WILL GO ON THE BACK COVER!

SET AGAINST THE DRAMATIC BACKDROP OF THE ANTEBELLUM SOUTH, "BELLES-A-POPPIN'" WEAVES A TALE OF TORRID LOVE BETWEEN **VICKI**, A FIERY LOUNGE SINGER, AND **LANCE**, A RUGGED TENNIS PRO!

AS REBEL SOLDIERS DUMP TEA IN THE ATLANTA HARBOR, VICKI FOLLOWS LANCE TO DISNEY WORLD, UNAWARE OF THE WACKY HIGH JINKS WHICH WILL ENSUE DURING A ZANY CHOLERA OUTBREAK!

"WACKY HIGH JINKS"?

CAR CRASHES, FOOD FIGHTS... STUFF LIKE THAT.

ANY ROMANCE NOVEL NEEDS A GOOD **COVER!** ANGIE, YOU AND I WILL POSE WHILE TEDDY TAKES SOME PHOTOS!

I DON'T WANT MY PICTURE ON THE COVER OF SOME BOOK!

IT WON'T BE! I'LL **PAINT** THE COVER! I JUST NEED SOME PHOTOS TO WORK FROM!

ALL THE BEST COVERS SHOW THE GIRL TEARING THE GUY'S SHIRT OFF! ANGIE, YOU GO AHEAD AND RIP MY SHIRT OFF! OOOOH, THIS'LL BE **HOT!**

OW! OW!

DON'T ASK.

I'M READY TO SEND MY ROMANCE NOVEL TO PUBLISHERS! I FINALLY FIGURED OUT HOW TO END IT!

ON THE EVE OF THEIR WEDDING DAY, OUR STAR-CROSSED LOVERS ARE TRAMPLED TO DEATH BY CRAZED BURROS WHILE TOURING THE GRAND CANYON!

SO YOU SEE, THEY'RE TOTALLY **DOOMED!** BEFORE THEIR LOVE CAN BLOOM, IT WITHERS AND DIES ON THE VINE!

A FITTING METAPHOR FOR YOUR LITERARY CAREER.

LATER, THEY COME BACK TO LIFE AS KICK-BOXING ZOMBIES...

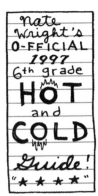

nate wright's
O-FFICIAL
1997
6th grade
HOT
and
COLD
Guide!
"★ ★ ★ ★"

HOT: Mr. Galvin!

Let's turn to page ZZZ...

He fell asleep again!

High-five me!

COLD: Duh.

I summon thee, demons of darkness!

Dang!

She's goin' postal!

HOT: Slides (recess)

WA-HOO!

COLD: Slides (biology)

Here's another example of cell division...

Sigh...

HOT: Hangin' out by your locker!

What's happenin', ladies?

♡Hiiiiiii

COLD: Hangin' out WITH your locker!

You are my only friend! SOB!

HOT: Bringing your own lunch from home!

Hey, HEY! Pizza and chips again!

HOW'S THE MEAT-LOAF?

COLD.

WHY DON'T YOU JUST BRING YOUR OWN LUNCH?

CHECK IT OUT! I BORROWED A VIDEO CAMERA FROM THE SCHOOL LIBRARY!

THE LIBRARIAN LET YOU BORROW THAT?

YUP!

SHE'S NEW, RIGHT?

YEAH, WITH ROOKIE FACULTY, YOU'VE GOT ABOUT A MONTH-LONG WINDOW OF OPPORTUNITY.

NATE WRIGHT, OFFICIAL VIDEOGRAPHER OF P.S. 38, AT YOUR SERVICE!

DO YOU **MIND**? I'M TRYING TO DO MY HOMEWORK!

HECK, NO, I DON'T MIND! BUT LET'S PUMP UP THE ENERGY A TAD, OK?

YOU'RE JUST **SITTING** THERE! I NEED **ACTION**! **GIVE** ME SOMETHING! **ANY**THING!

THERE'S A BIT OF IMPROVISATION THAT'LL END UP ON THE CUTTING ROOM FLOOR.

WANNA BE ON CANDID CAMERA, GUYS? YOU'RE LOOKING AT P.S. 38'S OFFICIAL SCHOOL VIDEOGRAPHER!

YOU'RE NOT AN OFFICIAL **ANYTHING**, NATE! YOU CAN'T JUST **APPOINT** YOURSELF SCHOOL VIDEOGRAPHER!

BLOW IT OUT YOUR EAR, SHEILA. YOU'RE JUST MAD **YOU** DIDN'T THINK OF IT **FIRST!**

OKAY, ENOUGH CHIT-CHAT! WE'RE ROLLING! DO SOMETHING SPONTANEOUS!

I HEREBY DECLARE A BLOODLESS COUP!

OOPS. IT **WAS** BLOODLESS!...

OW!

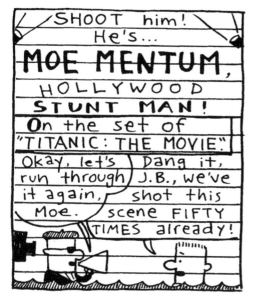

SHOOT him! He's...

~~MOE MENTUM~~,

HOLLYWOOD **STUNT MAN!**

On the set of "TITANIC: THE MOVIE."

Okay, let's run through it again, Moe.

Dang it, J.B., we've shot this scene FIFTY TIMES already!

Things keep going wrong! I'm beginning to believe what everyone's been saying: This movie is **JINXED!**

That's not true! In fact, the OPPOSITE is true!

We've got our very own GOOD LUCK CHARM here on the set! She's 98-year-old **GLADYS FRUMP,** an ACTUAL **SURVIVOR** of the REAL Titanic disaster back in 1912!!

With Gladys around, how can there be a jinx?

Good point, J.B.!

LOCUSTS

The Adventures Of...

MOE MENTUM,

★ HOLLYWOOD ★
STUNT MAN!!

On the set of
"TITANIC: THE MOVIE."

J.B., we just showed the movie to our test market audience!

Well, what'd they think? Do we have a hit on our hands?

With just a few minor changes, we will! There were a couple of parts the audience didn't like!

Which parts?

Well, they got a little bummed out when the ship actually sank.

I can't stand it...

Also, the whole 1912 thing didn't register. Can we update it to the bikini era?

DID YOU HEAR THAT JOKE I TOLD DURING MATH YESTERDAY? AM I A RIOT OR AM I A RIOT?

I JUST HAVE A GOD-GIVEN GIFT FOR AMUSING PEOPLE! A DAY WHEN I DON'T MAKE SOMEONE LAUGH IS A DAY **WASTED!**

YOUR FLY'S OPEN.

HA HA HA

THAT OUGHTA BE WORTH A WHOLE **WEEK!**

HA HA HA HA HA HA

Assignment 12:
Imagination-Building
Compose your own
obituary as it
might appear at
the end of your
life.

Nate Wright, internationally-
known cartoonist and
bon vivant, died Sunday.
The world mourned.

Wright, the genius
behind such hilarious
characters as "Doctor
Cesspool", "Moe Mentum,"
and "Dan Cupid, Love
Consultant," was, simply
put, a creative
supernova.

There
was little in
Wright's humble
beginnings to sug-
gest the dazzling
life of achievement
he would lead.

He overcame a laughably
small allowance, an exis-
tence devoid of cable TV,
and a sadistic older
sister on her way to
becoming a national
treasure.

**NATE! WHERE'S MY
DIARY?? YOU'VE BEEN
READING IT AGAIN,
YOU LITTLE WORM!**

YOU'RE DEAD!
DEAD!

Wright was
eleven years
old when his
life ended
violently...

WHAT'S ALL THIS?

JUST GETTING READY FOR HALLOWEEN.

WHOA, **WHOA!** YOU CAN'T HAND OUT THIS STUFF! THIS ISN'T EVEN **REAL CANDY!** IT'S THAT LAME **GENERIC** STUFF!

NATE, CANDY'S CANDY. BESIDES, BUYING THAT KIND SAVED ME ALMOST FIVE DOLLARS.

ADD MY HOUSE TO THE "EGG LIST."

MY DAD IS PLANNING TO HAND OUT **GENERIC CANDY** ON HALLOWEEN! CAN YOU BELIEVE THAT? CAN YOU **BELIEVE** IT?

IS **NOTHING** SACRED? CAN'T WE KIDS GO OUT TRICK-OR-TREATING AND EXPECT A QUALITY PRODUCT? APPARENTLY **NOT!** IT WON'T BE LONG UNTIL **OTHER** PARENTS FOLLOW THIS SORRY EXAMPLE!

HAS THE WHOLE WORLD GONE MAD??

I CAN'T SPEAK FOR THE WHOLE WORLD, BUT THERE ARE A FEW SQUARE FEET TO MY IMMEDIATE LEFT THAT COULD USE SOME HELP...

HERE, DAD. I WANT YOU TO HAND OUT COPIES OF THIS DISCLAIMER ON HALLOWEEN.

IT SAYS THAT EVEN THOUGH YOU, DAD, ARE GIVING OUT GENERIC CANDY, I, NATE, HAD ABSOLUTELY NOTHING TO DO WITH THIS SHAMEFUL DECISION!

AFTER ALL, I'VE GOT TO PROTECT MY REPUTATION!

YOU MISSPELLED FOUR WORDS IN THE FIRST SENTENCE ALONE.

I DID?

I'D SAY YOUR REPUTATION'S INTACT!

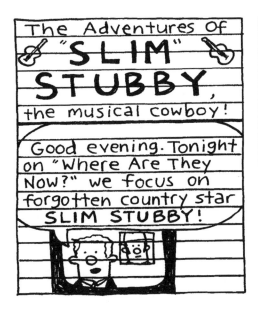

The Adventures Of "SLIM" STUBBY, the musical cowboy!

Good evening. Tonight on "Where Are They Now?" we focus on forgotten country star SLIM STUBBY!

Slim, once a household name in country music, saw his career dry up in the early eighties! He hasn't been seen or heard from since! Tonight... we SEARCH for Slim Stubby!

FILE PHOTO

We'll start here, at Slim's former recording studio!

Hi! Whatever happened to Slim Stubby?

Who?

Can we watch something else?

Hold it. Let's see if they're offering a reward.

MRS. GODFREY IS SUCH A **SOCIOPATH**! TODAY SHE—

NATE! **NATE!**

YOU PUT ME IN A VERY AWKWARD POSITION WHEN YOU GOSSIP ABOUT MY FELLOW TEACHERS! I DON'T WANT TO HEAR IT!

OKAY, MR. ROSA, I GOTCHA. FROM NOW ON, I'LL REFER TO HER SIMPLY AS "MADAME X."

I APPRECIATE YOUR DISCRETION.

ANYWAY, I'M FLIPPING THROUGH MADAME X'S DAY PLANNER, WHEN SUDDENLY...

CELEB-RITY chat!

Here's your host: *BIFF BIFFWELL!*

Hello, friends! I'm here once again with our old friend... **DAN CUPID!**

Howdy-ho, Biff!

Dan, I understand that today you'll be attempting something quite **CHALLENG-ING!**

Right you are!

I'll be trying to find a mate for every-one's favorite lonely bachelor... **DAD!**

What's the first step, Dan?

The first step is simply to fly around, looking for single women in Dad's general area!

Then, when you spot a likely prospect, you simply take aim... and **FIRE!**

SPROING!

Sounds fool-proof!

Oops! No, it's not fool-proof, Biff. In fact, I've just made a rather serious mistake.

What kind of mistake?

Bad aim. Ever heard that phrase, "puppy love"?

HEY! HEY! NO! DOWN!

CAN WE KEEP HIM, DAD? CAN WE KEEP HIM?

WELL, IT TURNS OUT THAT MY **GIRLFRIEND** IS A BETTER ARTIST THAN **I** AM!

IN **TWENTY MINUTES**, ANGIE CRANKED OUT A PAINTING THAT **I** COULDN'T DO IF I TRIED FOR TWENTY **YEARS!**

THAT'S GREAT, NATE!

YOU MUST BE VERY PROUD OF HER!

AS USUAL, HE COMPLETELY MISSED THE WHOLE POINT.

UH... ANGIE?

HI, NATE!

ANGIE, I...UH... NEVER REALLY TOLD YOU YESTERDAY HOW MUCH I LIKE YOUR PAINTING.

IT'S GREAT!... NO, IT'S **BETTER** THAN GREAT! IT'S A **MASTER-PIECE!**

THAT'S SO SWEET!

SO YOU THINK THAT REALLY LOOKS LIKE ELVIS?

OH, YEAH. YOU DID AN **AMAZ-ING** JOB ON THE SEQUINS!

...SO AT FIRST, I FELT A LITTLE **JEALOUS** THAT YOU'D DONE SUCH AN AWESOME PAINTING!

BUT FRANCIS HELPED ME SEE THAT SUCH A COMPETITIVE ATTITUDE ISN'T HEALTHY! NOW, I CAN ACCEPT THE FACT THAT WE'RE **BOTH** GOOD ARTISTS!

THAT'S GREAT, NATE! I'M GLAD!

SO, WANNA GO DO SOMETHING? WANNA PLAY CHESS?

UM... NOT REALLY.

MONOPOLY?

NO

YAHTZEE?

NO

WANNA THUMB-WRESTLE?

NATE! I THOUGHT I TOLD YOU TO GET THESE LEAVES RAKED!

AWWW, DAD!

I DON'T **WANT** TO RAKE THE LEAVES! DO I **HAVE** TO?

HMM... TELL YOU WHAT...

I'LL GIVE YOU THE CHANCE TO GET OUT OF IT! ALL YOU HAVE TO DO IS ANSWER ONE QUESTION!

WHAT KIND OF QUESTION?

OH, IT'S VERY STRAIGHTFORWARD! A SIMPLE TRUE-FALSE QUESTION!

HMM... TRUE-FALSE, EH?

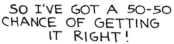

SO I'VE GOT A 50-50 CHANCE OF GETTING IT RIGHT!

I'LL TAKE THOSE ODDS! GO AHEAD!

OKAY. TRUE OR FALSE...

DAD HAD A **VERY** INTERESTING DISCUSSION WITH MRS. GODFREY WHEN HE RAN INTO HER AT THE GROCERY STORE THIS MORNING.

...SO THEN WHEN I GAVE MR. STAPLES THE DRAWING I'D DONE OF HIM, HE DIDN'T EVEN **CARE** THAT I HADN'T DONE MY HOMEWORK!

YOU SEE WHAT THIS **MEANS**? I'LL DRAW CARICATURES OF **ALL** THE TEACHERS! I MAY **NEVER** HAVE TO DO ANOTHER HOMEWORK ASSIGNMENT!

OF COURSE, I'VE GOT TO MAKE SURE THEY **LIKE** THE DRAWINGS! NOTHING LIKE A LITTLE FLATTERY, I ALWAYS SAY!

THINK THAT LOOKS LIKE MR. GALVIN?

THE HALO MIGHT BE A BIT MUCH.

HELLO, NATE! READY FOR ANOTHER GREAT HOOPS SEASON?

YOU BET, COACH!

I'M GOING TO BE A DIFFERENT PLAYER THIS YEAR! A LOT MORE **AGGRESSIVE**!

I'M GOING TO TAKE SOME OF THE TECHNIQUES I'VE LEARNED IN **OTHER** SPORTS AND APPLY THEM TO **BASKETBALL**!

YES, I SEE YOU'RE WEARING CLEATS.

WELL, I COULDN'T FIND ANY GOLF SPIKES THAT FIT ME...

NAB!

VETO!

YOU KNOW, THAT TRAMPOLINE WON'T BE THERE DURING ACTUAL GAMES.

Hello, friends, I'm **BIFF BIFFWELL**! You remember me from such TV specials as "**Real-Life Ugly Divorces**" and "**When Houseplants Die**"!

Well, tonight we'll travel to a world even **MORE** bizarre and unsettling! Yes, we'll see what occurs....

"**WHEN TEENS DATE**"!

brought to you by: *Clear-A-Skin*!

Let's meet a REAL teen-age couple: **ELLEN** and **GORDIE**!

Like countless young lovebirds, Ellen and Gordie **THINK** they have a lot in common!

I can't believe we BOTH like "Party Of Five"!

we BELONG together!

But beneath this superficial facade lurk a great many DIFFERENCES waiting to be exposed! The truth is: Ellen and Gordie's fairy-tale romance is a ticking **TIME BOMB**!

note: brain size

WHAT'S YOUR PROBLEM, BRAT? SCRAM!

HEY, I CAN HANG OUT HERE IF I WANT! IT'S **MY** HOUSE, TOO!

To see how long it takes for this "relationship" to unravel, we'll introduce an **EXTERNAL STRESS** into their environment! Watch what happens!

AW... LET HIM STAY.

OH, **THAT'S** NICE! TAKE **HIS** SIDE!

SIX... SEVEN... EIGHT...

Time Again For....
UP CLOSE AND PERSONAL!

Hello friends! CHIP CHIPSON here, talking with snow-meister JACK FROST!

T'sup, Chip?

I must confess, Jack, that I'm a little bit surprised by your appearance!

Why? WHY??

Because you thought I'd live in an IGLOO? Because you expected me to look all wintry and have ICICLES hanging off my nose??

Because you're not wearing pants.

Look... in this job, a man's got to stay cool.

THIS BASEMENT IS GOING TO BE "**PARTY CENTRAL!**" OVER HERE WILL BE THE STEREO... RIGHT HERE WILL BE THE DANCE AREA...

...AND OF COURSE, OVER IN THE CORNER, WE'LL HAVE A "COUPLES ONLY" AREA... ROWR!

MM-HMM... GOT AN AREA SET ASIDE FOR YOUR CHAPERON?

YEAH, I FIGURED YOU'D GO OUT FOR THE EVE-NING... YOU KNOW, GRAB A PIZZA, CATCH A MOVIE...

DREAM ON.

OKAY, OKAY, YOU CAN STAY IN THE LIVING ROOM. BUT YOU'VE GOT TO KNOCK BEFORE YOU COME DOWN-STAIRS.

349

WHAT ARE YOU DOING?

TAKING DOWN THESE PIC-TURES YOU'VE GOT HANGING EVERYWHERE.

DURING THIS PARTY, ALL MY CLASSMATES WILL BE HERE! YOU THINK I WANT THEM SEEING GOOFY BABY PICTURES OF ME WEAR-ING A DIAPER?

NOW, NATE, I REALLY THINK YOU'RE OVER—

HERE'S A FEW MORE TO GET RID OF.

THESE ARE OF YOUR SISTER.

IT'S A PARTY, NOT A FREAK SHOW. YOU WANT TO LOSE THOSE PERMANENT-LY, BE MY GUEST.

"CHEEZ DOODLES"? THESE ARE THE **ONLY** SNACK YOU'RE GOING TO SERVE AT YOUR PARTY?

HEY, WHAT MORE DO YOU NEED?

WELL, YOU MIGHT WANT TO SERVE STUFF THAT'S A BIT MORE... ELEGANT!

ELEGANT, EH?

HEY, HOW ABOUT **THIS**? WE'LL LET PEOPLE STAB THE CHEEZ DOODLES WITH THESE FANCY TOOTHPICKS! **THAT'S** PRETTY ELEGANT, RIGHT?

AMONG WHICH SPECIES?

PLUS!... ※ MUNCH ※ ※ MUNCH ※... AFTER A FEW DOZEN OF THESE BABIES, YOU **NEED** A TOOTHPICK!

I MUST SAY, I'M REALLY STARTING TO GET PSYCHED ABOUT YOUR PARTY!

YEAH... I GUESS.

WHAT'S THE MATTER? YOU KEEP SAYING HOW **AWESOME** IT'S GOING TO BE!

IT'S JUST THAT...

WELL, YOU SEE... I'VE NEVER... I'VE... UM.... I MEAN... BEFORE I MET ANGIE, I... THAT IS, I... UH...

CAN I SPEAK FRANKLY?

APPARENT- LY NOT.

WHAT IS **WITH** YOU? YOUR PARTY'S ABOUT TO START AND ALL YOU CAN DO IS **EAT!**

I CAN'T HELP IT! I EAT WHEN I GET NERVOUS!

THIS IS THE FIRST PARTY WHERE I'LL BE PART OF A **COUPLE!** I'M STRESSIN' OUT! I DON'T KNOW WHAT TO DO! AM I SUPPOSED TO MAKE OUT WITH ANGIE OR **WHAT?**

AND IF I **AM**, HOW DO I **DO** IT? WHAT DO I DO FIRST?

DING DONG! ♪

PRETTY MUCH THE EXACT OPPOSITE OF WHAT YOU'RE DOING NOW.

CHOMP! NARF NARF

I LIKE THE WAY YOU'VE DECORATED FOR YOUR PARTY, NATE!

THANKS! THANKS, ANGIE!

SAY, WHAT'S WITH ALL THOSE BEAN-BAG CHAIRS AND PILLOWS OVER IN THE CORNER?

HUH? OH, THAT'S... UH... WELL...

IT LOOKS LIKE A PLACE FOR COUPLES TO MAKE OUT!

POINK!

...AND... UM... WE'RE A COUPLE...

KILL THOSE LIGHTS!

WHAT DO MY STARTLED EYES BEHOLD
IN CLASSROOM TWO-FIFTEEN?
A LIVING GODDESS? OR, PERHAPS,
A GORGEOUS BEAUTY QUEEN?

BUT NO! 'TIS NEITHER OF THESE THINGS
WHICH STRIKES ME LIKE A DART.
'TIS MRS. GODFREY SITTING THERE.
BE STILL, MY FOOLISH HEART!

A TEACHER, YES... BUT SO MUCH MORE!
SHE WORKS AND NEVER RESTS.
THE TASK BEFORE HER AS WE SPEAK?
CORRECTING COUNTLESS TESTS.

AND SOMEWHERE IN
THAT TOWERING PILE,
MY TEST AWAITS HER PEN.
SHE'LL READ IT AND
DISCOVER THAT
I'VE SADLY FAILED AGAIN!

BUT NOT FOR LACK OF TRYING, NO!
A GALLANT TRY I MADE.
SHE'LL SAY, "AN EFFORT
SUCH AS THIS
DESERVES A BETTER GRADE!"

AN ANGEL MRS. GODFREY IS.
A SAINT, AND NOTHING LESS!
I'LL ASK HER, "DID I PASS THE TEST?"
AND SHE WILL ANSWER...

YOU HAVE GOT
TO BE KIDDING.

THERE'S NOTHING
I HATE MORE
THAN A POEM
THAT DOESN'T
RHYME.

OKAY, ANGIE'S GIVING OFF SOME POSITIVE VIBES HERE... SHE'S SUBTLY LETTING ME KNOW THAT SHE WANTS TO GET CLOSER...

NOW I'VE JUST GOT TO CASUALLY STEER HER OVER TOWARD "MAKE-OUT CORNER."

shuffa
shuffa
shuffa

GOTTA BE SUAVE ABOUT IT, THOUGH... JUST A LITTLE STROLL ACROSS THE ROOM... NO BIG DEAL... NOOOOOOO BIG DEAL...

WHA-?

HEY!

SORRY. DIBS ON THIS CHAIR.

WELL, NATE, ALL YOUR FRIENDS SEEM TO BE HAVING A GOOD TIME! YOU'VE PUT ON A GREAT PARTY!

OOP! WAS THAT THE DOORBELL? BETTER GO CHECK IT OUT!

NOW... WHERE WERE WE?

ANGIE, YOUR MOM'S HERE TO PICK YOU UP.

NO!

YOU'RE SCREWING UP MY FANTASY LIFE.

It's the P.S. 38 *Christmas* WISH LIST!

"" with your hosts: BIFF BIFFWELL & CHIP CHIPSON

Hello again, Christmas shoppers! Wondering what some of the 6th-grade teachers at P.S. 38 would like as gifts?

Let's take a look, Biff!

Here's MR. GALVIN, the biology teacher!

How about a new cap for his fountain pen?

Mrs. Blosser, cafeteria monitor?...

...A pair of size 12 triple-E golf shoes!

SLIPPA SLIPPA SLIPPA

COACH CALHOUN, hoops guru, would like...

...a MEGAPHONE!

PASS the ball! **PASS** it!... Hey! NO! **DON'T SHOOT**!... I said **DON'T**... Dag-nab it!

What does Mr. Staples, the math teacher, need?

How about a life?

...and then the duck says to the camel: "No, I said a HEXAGON!" Ha Ha! Hee!

...And now how about MRS. GODFREY social studies teacher?

Good question, Biff! What will **SHE** ask for this Christmas?

YOUR RESEARCH PAPER, PLEASE.

OH, WAS THAT DUE TODAY?

Hello again, friends... I'm Biff Biffwell. Tonight on "Up Close And Personal," we focus on a man who truly exemplifies this joyous time of year: **SANTA CLAUS!**

Santa is adored by millions, but he remains a **mysterious** figure! As you might expect, he declined to be interviewed for this story.

FILE PHOTO

So instead, we've assembled a portrait of the man **BEHIND** the myth! We've spoken with dozens of people who knew him **BEFORE** he achieved worldwide fame!

Yes, tonight we bring you...

SANTA: UNCOVERED!

The crushed-velvet pantsuit didn't bother me... but when he started hanging out with elves... well...

Santa's Mother

cont'd

SANTA: UNCOVERED!!

Years before he became an international star, Santa was just a normal kid! **EDDIE MAC-GREGOR** was Santa's best friend!

To me, he was always "Nick."

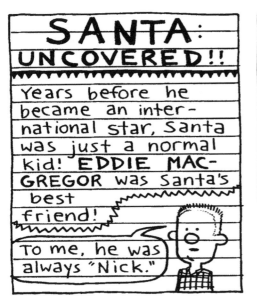

He liked to play ball, go fishing, stuff like that! There was never even the slightest hint that he'd be famous one day!

But then, when he started to hit the big time... well, you could see it happening! He got conceited! Success started to go to his head!

When did you realize things had changed?

When he put that "Saint" in front of his name. That tipped me off.

cont'd!

PSST! TEDDY!

WOW! LOOK AT ALL THOSE SNOWBALLS!

SSH! I DON'T WANT FRANCIS TO HEAR US!

HAVING A SNOWBALL FIGHT WITH FRANCIS, EH?

"FIGHT"? THIS IS NO MERE **FIGHT!**

A **FIGHT** IS JUST A COUPLE GUYS HUCKING SNOWBALLS AT EACH OTHER! **THIS** IS OUT-AND-OUT **WARFARE!**

THERE'S REAL **STRATEGY** INVOLVED HERE! WE'VE GOT HEADQUARTERS! WE'VE GOT BATTLE PLANS!

WE'VE GOT CACHES OF AMMO! DEMILITARIZED ZONES! TRENCHES! FOX-HOLES! BOOBY TRAPS!

POW!

...DOUBLE AGENTS!

HIGH-FIVE ME, MY LOYAL FOOT SOLDIER!

Peirce

Big Nate is distributed internationally by Andrews McMeel Syndication.

Big Nate's Greatest Hits copyright © 2015 by United Feature Syndicate, Inc. All rights reserved. Printed in China. No part of this book may be used or reproduced in any manner whatsoever without written permission except in the case of reprints in the context of reviews.

Andrews McMeel Publishing
a division of Andrews McMeel Universal
1130 Walnut Street, Kansas City, Missouri 64106

www.andrewsmcmeel.com

19 20 21 22 23 SDB 13 12 11 10 9

ISBN: 978-1-4494-6489-9

Library of Congress Control Number: 2014947175

Made by:
King Yip (Dongguan) Printing & Packaging Factory Ltd.
Address and location of manufacturer:
Daning Administrative District, Humen Town
Dongguan Guangdong, China 523930
9th Printing—8/19/19

Big Nate can be viewed on the Internet at
www.gocomics.com/big_nate.

These strips appeared in newspapers from January 1, 1997, to December 31, 1997, and were also in the ebooks, *Big Nate Makes a Splash*, *Big Nate: Dibs on This Chair*, and *Big Nate: Pray for a Fire Drill*.

Check out these and other books from Andrews McMeel Publishing

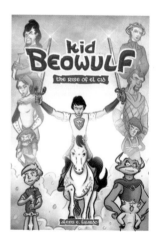